contents

For Isla
J.D.

For Grandad Pop
L.R.

The Quick Brown Fox Cub

Illustrated by Lucy Richards

 # A New Home

Frisk was a quick brown fox cub. He lived with his mother, his brother and his sister in a home called

The Old Burrow
The Tree Roots
The Edge of the Wood
The Country.

Frisk was a big worry to his mother. He was always running off by himself to look for rabbits.

How many times do I have to tell you?

Sorry, Mum.

'Why can't you stay and play with the others?' Mum scolded him. 'Do you want the fox-hunters to catch you like they caught your dad?'

'Sorry, Mum,' Frisk said, but a minute later he was off again.

In the end Mum was so worried that one evening she told the cubs, 'We're moving to town.'

'What's town?' Frisk asked.

'It's a nice place with no hunters,' said Mum. 'I used to live there before I met your dad.'

Let's go!

'Does town have rabbits?' asked Frisk.

'We won't need rabbits. There's lots of other food in town,' said Mum.

So that night the cubs followed Mum
to town. But when they got there, Frisk
felt scared. 'You were wrong, Mum,'
he said. 'There are hunters here! Great big
ones with round legs.'

'It's all
right, they can't
smell us,' said Mum. 'As long
as you don't run into the road you'll be safe.'
Mum led the cubs to a bramble patch by
some silvery lines, and
started to dig.

But just then a huge long monster came roaring towards them.

'Help! Another hunter!' cried Frisk.

'This kind can't smell either,' said Mum, and the monster roared on past them, along the silvery lines.

So now Frisk and his family were town foxes. Their new home was called

The New Burrow
The Brambles
The Railway Bank
Town.

Magic Rabbits

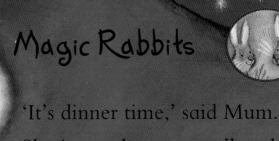

'It's dinner time,' said Mum.

She jumped over a wall and the cubs followed her. They landed in a garden with a wooden table in the middle of it.

'What's that?' asked Frisk.

'It's a fox table,' said Mum.

On top of the table the foxes found some bread and bacon rinds. They ate them all up.

Fox food!

'What's for pudding?' asked Frisk.

'Follow me,' said Mum, and she took them
to a big black bin.

'It's a fox bin,' she told them. She nosed the
lid off it and they found some more fox food
inside, as well as some nice cans for the cubs
to play with. They ate and played till the sky
began to grow light.

'It's bedtime,' said Mum.
'I don't want to go to bed.
I want to do some more
exploring,' said Frisk,
but Mum told him he
would have to wait.
    'Nights are for exploring.
        Days are for sleeping,'
            she said, and she led
                the cubs back to their new
                    home in the bramble patch.

Frisk woke up before the others. It was still light, but he couldn't wait to go exploring again. He left Mum and the others sleeping, and jumped over the wall into the garden.

Near the fox bin he saw a door with a flap in the bottom of it.

'It must be a fox flap!' said Frisk. He nosed it open and bounded through it into a room. There was a bowl of fox food on the floor. Frisk ate it all up. It tasted even better than the food on the fox table or in the fox bin.

Just then he heard a voice. 'Thanks for joining us on Fur and Feathers,' it said. 'Today we're looking at rabbits.'

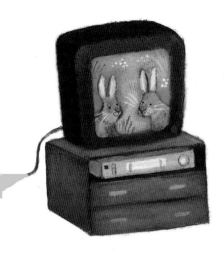

Rabbits! That sounded good. Frisk padded towards the voice, into another room. A girl was sitting on a chair with a cat on her lap.

The cat was asleep, but the girl was watching a big square shiny box.

Frisk looked at the box too. It was full of
rabbits! He let out a yelp of excitement.
Then three things happened at once.

The cat
jumped down,

the girl
turned round,

and the rabbits in the
box turned into a man!

Frisk ran. He bounded through the fox flap and all the way back to his new home. He pounced on his sister to wake her up.

Hey, listen!

Go back to sleep.

'Mum was wrong. There are rabbits in town,' he told her. 'Magic ones that can turn into people!'

'Don't be silly – it was just a dream,' said his sister.

12

 Magic Marks

That night the foxes ate and played in
the garden again. Just as they were about
to go home to bed, they heard one of the
round-legged hunters stop outside the house.

'Help! Maybe they can smell us after all!'
said Frisk. But Mum didn't look scared. 'That
sounds like a fox van to me,' she said, and she
led the cubs round to the front of the house.
The fox van had driven off, but on the front
doorstep stood three cartons.

'What's inside them?' asked Frisk.

'Fox milk,' said Mum. She bit a hole in one
of the cartons and tipped it over. The milk
ran out and the foxes lapped it up.

13

Frisk noticed that there
was a flap in the front door
too – but it was too small
and too high up to go through.

'That's a silly fox flap,' he said.
Just then the door opened and out came
the girl who had been watching the magic
box. She had a bag on her back.

The other foxes ran away, but Frisk wondered where the girl was going. He followed her along the road, keeping clear of the roaring hunters.

The girl went into a big building. Lots of other children were going into it too. Frisk hid and waited till they were all inside. Then he crept to a window and looked in.

He saw some children sitting down and a woman standing up. The woman drew something on a black board with a small white stick. Frisk felt excited – it was a picture of a fox jumping over a dog! Then the woman made some strange marks on the board. They looked like this:

'That sentence has every letter of the alphabet in it,' said the woman.

'What is she talking about?' Frisk wondered.

'Now, Jenny,' said the woman. 'Point to the word "fox".'

A girl stood up. It was the one Frisk had followed! She went to the board and pointed to some of the marks.

'F – O – X. Fox,' said Jenny.

'Those marks mean me!' thought Frisk, and he ran home to tell his family.

The other cubs were asleep, but Mum lay
with one eye open.

'What time of day do you call this?' she
asked Frisk.

'Sorry Mum,' said Frisk. 'But I've been
exploring. And I've seen some magic marks.'

Mum wasn't interested in the marks. 'I keep
telling you,' she scolded him, 'nights are for
exploring. Days are for sleeping.'

 # Magic Ducks

Although Frisk was the last to bed, once again he was the first one up. He felt hungry. Remembering the fox food inside the house, he bounded over the wall, across the garden and through the fox flap.

There on the floor was the bowl of fox food, but the cat was eating it! When she saw Frisk she hissed at him.

Hiss!

Just then he heard a voice. 'Thanks for joining us on Fur and Feathers,' it said. 'Today, we're looking at ducks.'

Ducks! That sounded almost as good as rabbits. Frisk padded into the room with the magic box.

Jenny was watching it, and a dog was curled up at her feet. Frisk was scared of dogs, but this one was asleep.

This time, the magic box was full of ducks.

'I must keep quiet,' thought Frisk, but when one of the ducks quacked he couldn't help running towards it. Again, three things happened at once.

The dog
woke up,

the girl
turned round,

and the ducks
turned into a woman!

Woof!
Woof!

The dog
barked and Frisk
ran. He raced out of the room,
into the other room and towards the fox
flap. The dog was coming after him. Frisk
could hear him panting.

Frisk bounded through the fox flap. He
hoped that the dog would be too big to get
through. He felt his heart beating as he ran
across the garden and back over the wall to
the bramble patch.

Mum and the others were
still asleep. He bit his brother's
ear to wake him up. 'I've been hunted,' he
told him. 'And I've seen some magic ducks.'

'Don't be silly – it was just a dream,' said
his brother.

Zzzzzz...

That night, Frisk felt tired. While the others were still eating and playing in the garden he slunk back to bed. He woke up when they returned in the morning.

'You've missed the fox milk,' his brother told him.

'You are silly, muddling up night and day,' said his sister.

Then the two of them snuggled up to Mum and went to sleep.

By now Frisk was wide awake. He decided
to go and see if there was any fox milk
still left on the doorstep.

There wasn't, but he was just in time to see
Jenny come out of the house with her bag on
her back.

Frisk started to think about
the magic white marks.
'I must see them again, I must!' he
thought, and he followed Jenny
to the big building.

Over
here!

Me!
Me!

Jenny went inside
with all the other children,
but this time a lot of them
came back out again and
started to run around. They
seemed to be hunting a ball. A man was
holding a silver thing which he kept
blowing. 'It must be a hunting
horn,' thought Frisk.

Frisk went round to the back of the
building and found a whole row of fox bins,
full of good things. He poked his nose into a
big can and licked the food from the bottom
of it. Then he tried to get his nose out.

Help!

'Help! I'm stuck!' he said.
He couldn't see. He ran round and
round. Now he could hear voices
and feet all around him. The hunters!
He didn't know which way to run.

Then a voice said, 'Keep still, it's all right,' and Frisk felt the can being pulled off his nose.

Let me help you.

He could see now. Jenny was holding the can, and all the children were smiling. But the huntsman was looking at him through a big black thing. Help! Perhaps it was a gun.

Frisk ran home. His brother and sister were fast asleep, but Mum had been waiting up for him.

'How many times do I have to tell you?' she began. 'Days are for . . .'

'Sleeping. I know, and I'm sorry,' said Frisk. 'But I did so want to see the magic marks again.' Then he told Mum all about his adventure.

Mum was still cross, but she said, 'I don't think the black thing was a gun.'

'What was it then?' asked Frisk.

'A fox-watcher,' said Mum.

The Lazy Dog

In the end, Mum gave up trying to stop Frisk muddling up night and day. He just couldn't keep away from the big building. He went there every day and looked through the window. He watched the woman making the magic marks on the board and the children telling her what they meant. He learnt that the marks were called letters, and he learnt to read them.

'I can read "The quick brown fox jumps over the lazy dog",' he told Mum proudly one night. 'That's got all the letters of the alphabet in it.'

Sometimes the big and small people saw him, but Frisk didn't mind, as long as they didn't come too near. He didn't even mind when they looked at him through the strange black fox-watcher.

Frisk longed to watch the magic box again. When he looked through Jenny's window he could only see the back of it. But he was too scared to go through the fox flap again, in case he met the dog.

Ruff! Ruff!

Now and then the foxes saw the dog in the garden. Sometimes he was hunting a ball or a stick which Jenny threw for him, but more often he was asleep. He was rather a lazy dog. Even so, Mum said it was best to keep away from him.

Frisk also kept away from the two big people who shared Jenny's house with her. He didn't like them as much as Jenny. He couldn't understand why they let birds sit on the fox table, or why they let the cat come and go through the fox flap. Even worse, they stole the fox milk for themselves unless the foxes got there first.

That's my milk!

One morning, when the foxes were waiting
by the front door for the fox milk to arrive,
Frisk noticed a paper thing sticking out of
the silly high-up fox flap. He pulled it out.

'What's this?' he asked, but for once
Mum didn't know.

'Look! There's a picture of the magic box on the front!' said Frisk. He looked inside and saw a lot of pictures and writing.

'I can read this!' he said proudly. But most of it was boring stuff about people.

Then Frisk saw some words which made his bushy tail swish.

It sounded very exciting, but what did it mean?

Just then, Jenny came out of the house and
Frisk followed her to the big building. He
looked through the window and saw the
woman writing on the board:

Today 5 o'clock Fox Watch.

It's tonight!

'Don't forget to watch the box!'
she said to the children.
Suddenly, Frisk understood. There
were going to be foxes in the magic box!
'I must see them, I must!' he cried.

The Quick Brown Fox Club

Frisk was so excited that he hardly slept a wink all day. When the others were still asleep he bounded over the wall, ran to Jenny's back door and poked his nose through the fox flap. But there he stopped. He didn't dare go any further. He was scared of meeting the dog and being hunted again.

Where's the dog?

Just then, Jenny came into the
room and saw him peeping through
the fox flap. She put a finger on
her lips and beckoned to him.

Frisk decided to be brave.
He jumped through the fox flap.

Ssshh!

'Come on, Jenny, it's starting!' he heard
one of the big people call, and then
he heard another voice saying,
'Tonight we're looking at foxes.'

Frisk crept after Jenny into the room with the magic box. The two big people were already watching it. Jenny sat down with them. The cat jumped on to her lap. Frisk looked around and felt glad that he couldn't see the dog.

Where are the foxes?

He sat behind a chair and watched the magic box. But he couldn't see any foxes. There was a man talking. 'Teachers and children from schools up and down the country have taken part in this study,' the man was saying. What was he talking about?

Then suddenly, the man changed into a fox!
The fox was walking on a roof. Next, Frisk
saw some fox cubs playing in an empty house,
and some other ones eating from a fox bin.

And then he saw something even more
exciting. It was a fox cub with its head stuck
in a can. A lot of children were crowding
round the cub.

'Look, that's me!' said Jenny, and in the
magic box Frisk saw her pulling the can off
the fox cub's nose. Frisk's tail began to swish
with excitement – he was looking at himself!

He saw himself again and again – looking through the window of the big building, trotting along the railway bank, and playing with the other cubs in the bramble patch. Then he saw Mum tipping over the fox milk and his brother and sister eating from the fox table.

We're on the magic box!

Frisk's tail swished harder than ever, and it knocked something off a little table.

Once more, three things happened
at once.

The cat
jumped down,

the people
turned round,

and the foxes
turned into children!

Frisk ran out
of the room. He
bounded through
the other room,
towards the fox flap.

But lying on the
floor in front of
the fox flap was
the dog.

Frisk didn't have time to think. There was
only one thing to do.

'The quick brown fox jumps
over the lazy dog!' he said,
and he jumped.

The dog woke up and barked, but it was too
late. Frisk was already out through the fox
flap. He was on his way home to tell Mum
and the others that they were all magic foxes.

THE WRONG KIND OF BARK

Illustrated by Garry Parsons

For Hamish
and Jeddah
J.D.

For Christopher
and Emma
G.P.

Finlay and the Fish

Finlay sat next to the fish tank. He liked watching the fish. They were more interesting than the teacher.

There was a little bridge at the bottom of the fish tank. But the fish never swam under it. Or maybe they did when Finlay wasn't looking.

The big fish was swimming very near the bridge now.

'Go on!' Finlay whispered. 'Swim under it!'

The teacher was talking to the class.
'Tomorrow, I want you all to bring in a
flower for the nature table,' she said. 'It can
be any kind of flower.'

Finlay watched the big fish. It swam over
the bridge.

'Finlay!' said the teacher.
'What did I just say?'
'Any kind of
flower,' said Finlay.
'Yes,' said the
teacher. 'And
stop staring at
the fish!'

Any kind
of flower.

The Wrong Kind of Flower

'Did you all remember to bring in a flower?' asked the teacher next day.

Most of the class had.

Me, Miss!

Sally Wong had
a marigold.

David Simmons
had a rose. A lot of
it had been eaten
by greenfly.

Ruth Goodchild
had a pansy. She
had some extra
flowers for the
teacher too.

I grew it
myself.

The teacher filled a jamjar with water. She put it on the nature table. 'Now, all put your flowers in here,' she said.

Sally Wong put in the marigold.

What now Ruth?

David Simmons put in what was left of
the rose.

Ruth Goodchild put in the pansy.

'Please, Miss,' she said. 'Look what
Finlay's doing.'

The teacher looked at Finlay. He was
pouring some white stuff out of a bag into
the water.

'What are you doing, Finlay?' asked
the teacher.

'Putting my flour in the water, like you
said, Miss,' said Finlay.

Hey!
Stop!

'That's the wrong kind of flour,' said the
teacher. She had to change the water.

Later on, Finlay was watching the fish again. The little one was swimming very near the bridge.

'Go on!' whispered Finlay. 'Swim under it!'

You can do it!

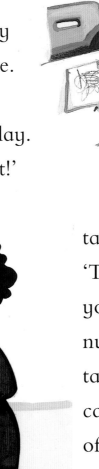

The teacher was talking to the class. 'Tomorrow, I want you all to bring in a nut for the nature table,' she said. 'It can be any kind of nut.'

Finlay watched the little fish. It swam around the bridge.

'Finlay!' said the teacher. 'What did I just say?'

'Any kind of nut,' said Finlay.

'Yes,' said the teacher. 'And stop staring at the fish!'

The Wrong Kind of Nut

'Did you all remember to bring in a nut?' asked the teacher next day.

Most of the class had.

Sally Wong had a walnut.

David Simmons had a conker. It had got a bit broken in a fight.

Ruth Goodchild had a coconut. She had a packet of peanuts for the teacher too.

'Now, put them all on the nature table,'
said the teacher.

Sally Wong put down the walnut.

David Simmons put down the
broken conker.

Miss!
Miss!

Ruth Goodchild
put down the
coconut.

'Please, Miss,' she
said. 'Finlay's putting
some metal things on
the table. That's not
what you said, Miss,
is it?'

'What are those, Finlay?' said the teacher.

'They're nuts, like you said, Miss,' said Finlay. 'My dad was screwing some into some shelves and he let me have these ones.'

'That's the wrong kind of nut,' said the teacher.

She moved Finlay to a different table. 'Now you can stop staring at the fish,' she said.

Try and concentrate, Finlay.

'Right,' said the teacher. 'It's time to practise our play.'

The class was doing a play about Nature. Some children had made masks.

Sally Wong had a daisy mask.

Finlay had a tomato mask.

David Simmons had a yellow mask. He was being the sun. He had cut one eye bigger than the other, but the teacher said it didn't matter.

Some children were being raindrops. They had long paper ribbons tied to their arms. The ribbons were supposed to be the rain.

Ruth Goodchild was Mother Nature. She had a wand and was allowed to boss everybody about.

The children practised the play in the hall. Then they came back to the classroom.

Finlay's new table was by the window. There was some scaffolding up outside. Some builders were going to do some work on the school roof. They were sitting on the scaffolding having their lunch. One of them had dropped a bit of his sandwich. A bird was hopping towards it.

'Go on,' whispered Finlay. 'Get it!'

The teacher was talking to the class.

'I want you all to bring in part of a tree for the nature table,' she said. 'It can be a twig, or a leaf, or a little bit of bark.'

Finlay watched the bird. It flew away.

'Finlay!' said the teacher. 'What did I just say?'

'Bring in bark,' said Finlay.

'Yes,' said the teacher. 'And stop staring out of the window.'

The Wrong Kind of Bark

The teacher came into the classroom the next day.

There were a lot of children round Finlay's table.

Miss! Miss!

'Please, Miss,' said Ruth Goodchild. 'Finlay's got a dog. That's not what you said, Miss, is it?'

Finlay had a small puppy in his arms.

'Finlay, you can't bring pets to school,' said the teacher.

'But you said to bring in a bark, Miss,' said Finlay. The puppy barked loudly.

'That's the wrong kind of bark,' said the teacher.

She phoned Finlay's home to see if his mum or dad could come for the puppy. But no one was in.

The teacher went back into the classroom.

The puppy was standing on the nature table. He was barking at the builders.

The jar of flowers was on its side. Most of the nuts were on the floor.

'Take him off the table, Finlay,' said the teacher. She cleared up the mess.

The puppy went on and on barking at the builders. Finlay put his anorak under the nature table.

'What are you doing now, Finlay?' asked the teacher.

'I'm making a bed for the puppy,' said Finlay. The puppy lay down on the anorak. He stopped barking.

'Now it's time to do the play for the rest of the school,' said the teacher.

The children put on their masks.

Sally Wong put on her daisy mask.

It's hot in here.

David Simmons put on his sun mask.

Finlay put on his tomato mask.

How do I tie this?

The puppy started to bark again. He
barked and barked at the tomato mask.

'He doesn't like the tomato mask,' said
Finlay. 'He thinks it's attacking me.'

'Take the mask off,' said the teacher. 'You
can put it on when we're down in the hall.'

Finlay took off
the tomato mask.
The puppy growled.
He grabbed
the mask in his
mouth and tore
it up.

Stop it!

The teacher was very cross. 'I'll have to tie
him up,' she said. She
found some string.
She tied one end of
it to the puppy's
collar. Then she
tied the other
end round a leg
of Finlay's table.

Finlay had to make a new tomato mask. There wasn't time for the paint to dry.

The teacher put the paint pot up on a shelf. Then they went down to the hall to act the play to the rest of the school.

The puppy was left alone in the classroom.

The builders were banging on the roof. The puppy barked at them. The builders went on banging. The shelves on the wall started to shake. They shook and shook. The pot of red paint jumped on the shelf. It fell on its side. The red paint started to run out of it . . .

Tomato Trouble

Down in the hall the children were doing their play. The children being flowers and fruit were curled up on the stage.

Ruth Goodchild was sitting in a chair with tinsel tied on it. It was her throne. 'Pitter patter raindrops,' she said. She waved her wand.

The children being raindrops ran on to the stage. They shook the ribbons on their arms. They were supposed to be watering the flowers and fruit.

David Simmons came on to the stage in his
sun mask. He stood stiffly over the plants.
From far off came a barking sound.
'Grow, plants, grow,' said Ruth.

The children being flowers and fruit began to uncurl. Finlay uncurled. The red paint from his tomato mask dripped down his jumper.

Grow, plants, grow.

The barking grew louder and louder.

'Grow taller,' said Ruth.

The flowers and fruit grew. Most of them grew slowly.

But the tomato shot up. It was still dripping
red paint. The tomato jumped off the stage.
It ran through the hall and up the stairs.

Ruth Goodchild looked cross.

The Right Kind of Bark

The teacher went out of the hall. Quietly, she followed the tomato up the stairs.

Finlay went into the classroom. The teacher followed him.

What's going on?

The puppy had stopped barking at the
builders. He was barking at the fish tank.
He was barking and barking and barking.

On the shelf the pot of red paint lay on its side. Red paint was running out of it. A few drops had dripped into the fish tank.

'Quick!' said the teacher. 'Bring me a jamjar of water, Finlay.' She took the paint pot off the shelf and put it on her table.

There was a net next to the fish tank. The teacher fished the big fish out of the tank.

Finlay and the puppy watched. The puppy had stopped barking.

The teacher tried to fish out the little fish. But it was a very fast swimmer. It kept swimming away.

'Yes!' said Finlay. The little fish was swimming under the bridge!

The teacher held the net the other side of the bridge and the little fish swam into it.

The teacher took the fish into the classroom next door. They had a fish tank too. She put the fish in it.

CLASS THREE'S FISH

'Now we'll have to change the water in our tank,' she said. 'We can't have the fish swallowing red paint.'

Later on, the other children came back to the classroom.

Ruth Goodchild still looked cross.

'I'm sorry I missed the end of the play,' said the teacher. 'But in a way I'm glad. If all the paint had gone into the water, the fish could be dead. What a good thing that Finlay's puppy warned us.'

Finlay cuddled his puppy.

'Perhaps it was the right kind of bark after all,' he said.